Farmer Dillo
Shapes Things Up

Jesse Adams

Pictures by Julie Speer
and Bruce Polhamus

JOURNEYFORTH

Greenville, South Carolina

Written by Jesse Adams
Illustration concepts: Julie Speer
3D illustrations by Unusual Films: Bruce Polhamus, David Rogers, John Murray
Design: Rita Golden

© 2009 by BJU Press
Greenville, SC 29614
JourneyForth Books is a division of BJU Press

ISBN 978-1-59166-865-7

15   14   13   12   11   10   9   8   7   6   5   4   3   2   1

To my wife and best friend,
Michelle
-JA

To Andre, Abigail, and Nathaniel
who surround me with love and fun!
-JS

To my wife, Laura
-BP

Hi everyone!
It is spring in Sundown.

Farmer Dillo is ready
for the new season.

He looks around his farm, but something is wrong.

Farmer Dillo says, "**Hmm. My farm is in bad shape. I need to do some work.**"

Farmer Dillo walks around his farm. He stops at his fence. But the fence is broken!

"That is not right," he says.
"The fence is the wrong shape."

Can you tell **what shape** the fence is now?

Farmer Dillo says, "My fence should not be a **triangle**. It should be a **rectangle**."

So Farmer Dillo uses his hammer and fixes the fence.

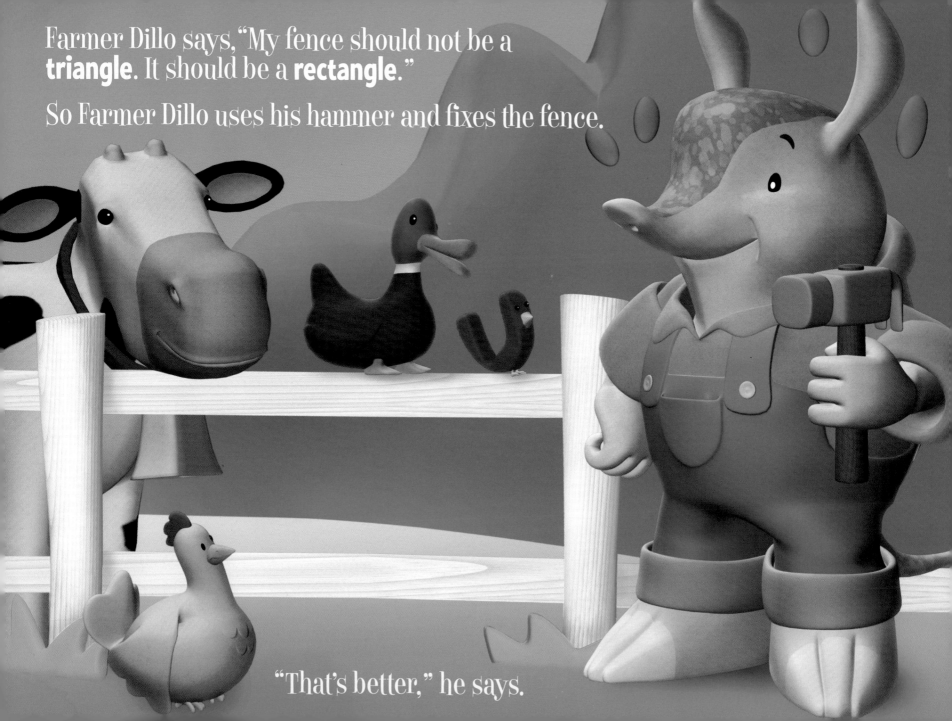

"That's better," he says.

Then Farmer Dillo walks over to his barn. His ladder needs fixing. "That is not right," he says. "This step makes the wrong shape."

Can you tell **what shape** the step makes now?

Farmer Dillo says, "My ladder's step should not make a **rectangle**. It should make a **square**."

So Farmer Dillo uses his screwdriver to fix the step on his ladder.

"That's better," he says.

Then Farmer Dillo walks to his pond. The pond is full of weeds!

"That is not right," he says. "My pond is the wrong shape."

Can you tell **what shape** the pond is now?

Farmer Dillo says, "My pond should not form a **square**. It should form an **oval**." So Farmer Dillo uses his shears and cuts the weeds in his pond.

"That's better," he says.

Next Farmer Dillo walks to his tractor. The tire is flat!

"That is not right," he says. "The tractor tire is the wrong shape."

Can you tell **what shape** the tractor tire is now?

Farmer Dillo says, "My tractor tire cannot be an **oval**. It must be a **circle**."

So Farmer Dillo uses his pump and fixes his tractor tire.

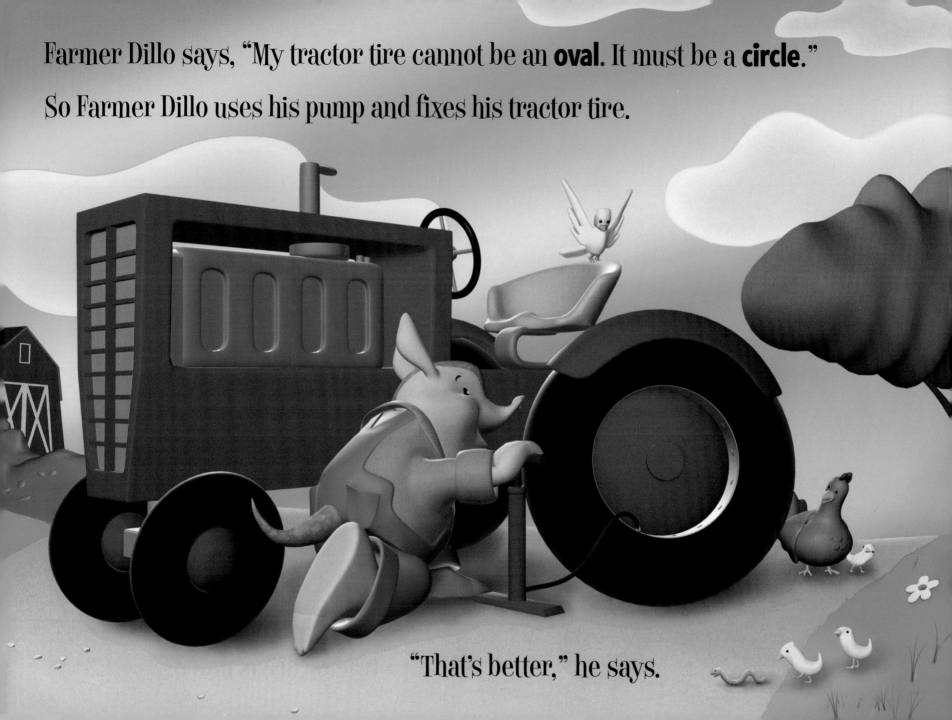

"That's better," he says.

But when Farmer Dillo looks down at his overalls, he sees a hole in his knee!

"That is not right," he says. "My overalls are in bad shape."

What shape is the hole in Farmer Dillo's overalls?

Farmer Dillo says, "My overalls should not have a **circle** in them.
I will patch the hole with this **diamond**."

So Farmer Dillo uses his needle and thread and fixes
the hole in his overalls.

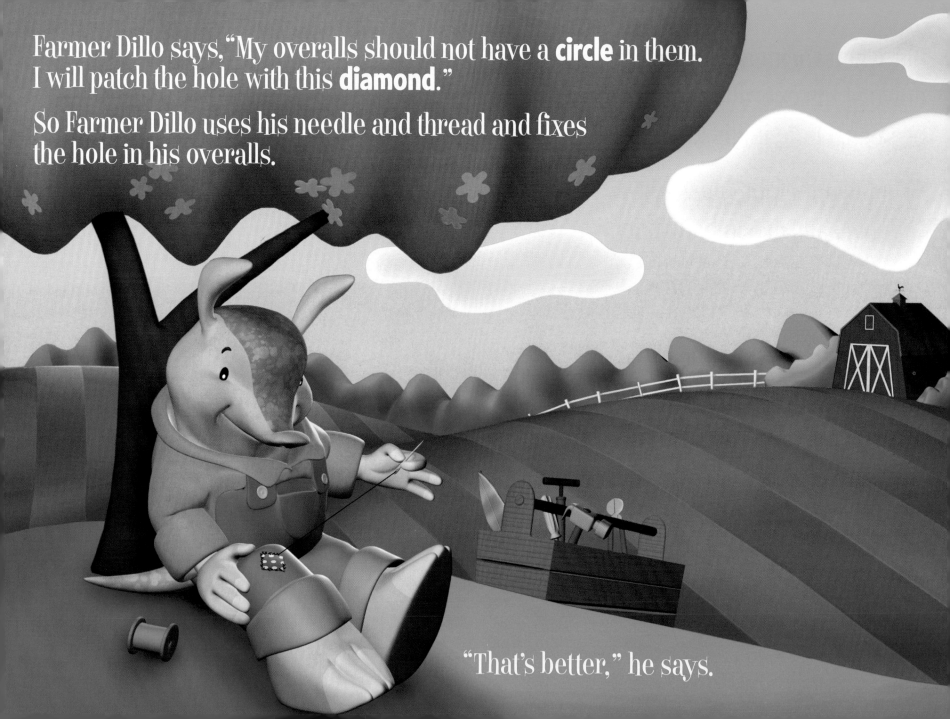

"That's better," he says.

So Farmer Dillo walks back to his house.
He stops at his bush. But it is not trimmed!

"That is not right," he says.
"My bush is the wrong shape."

Can you tell **what shape**
his bush is now?

Farmer Dillo says, "My bush should not make a **diamond**. It should make a **triangle**."

So Farmer Dillo uses his clippers and fixes his bush.

"That's better," he says.

Then the sun sets, and the moon comes out. The moon is not full!

"**That is not right**," he says.
"The moon is the wrong shape."

Can you tell **what shape** the moon is now?

Farmer Dillo says,
"The moon should not be a **crescent**.
It should be a **circle**."

So Farmer Dillo uses his hammer to fix the moon,
but he cannot fix it.

He tries his screwdriver.
He tries his shears.
He tries his pump.
He tries his needle and thread.
He tries his clippers to fix the moon.

He cannot fix the moon!
But that's OK . . .

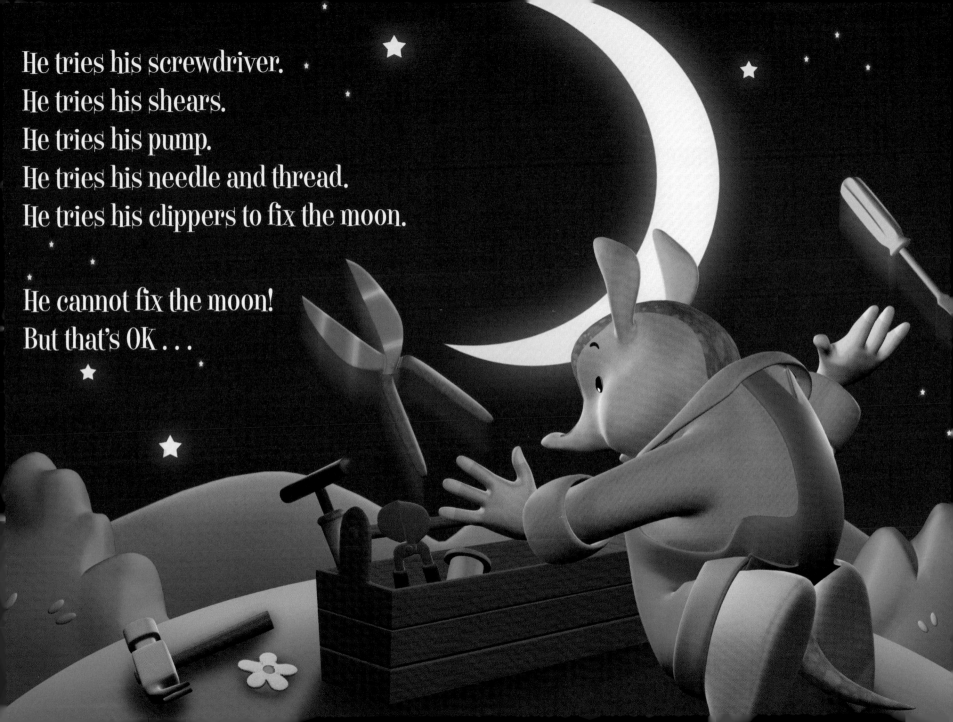

The sun's coming up anyway.
Good morning, Farmer Dillo!